CYMRU AM BYTH

POEMS ABOUT WALES AND BEING WELSH

1. EISTEDDFOD DAYS

The Singing of glories

Competitions and performances

Welshness and unity

Canon Lan

Welsh is best

Wales for ever

Cymru am byth

Mae Hen Wlad Fy Nhadau

Hundreds of tents pavilions and booths

Open spaces

Welsh spoken everywhere

Come celebrate

Come celebrate

We are Welsh and proud

Being Welsh matters

Children dancing

Harp's being strung

The chairing ceremony

We love our poets

Druids and dancers

The Gorsedd of Bards

Stone circles and icons

All part of the ceremony

Fun flavour and festival

The thrill of the main pavilion

The thrill of the song

The thrill of the dance

Children steal our hearts in the song and the dance

2. Saint David's Day

Our patron saint

It's March the 1st

Dewi Sant

Schools and bunting

Festivals and chorus

Traditional dress

Traditional song

Dancing and poems and teachers directing

Children do their best and everyone claps

Claps and cheers

Giggles and laughter

Daffodils and leeks pinned to the chest

Traditions alive again

Happy St David's day

Greeting on streets

Flags and dragons everywhere

Welsh spirit is soaring in the air

Not a National holiday but it should be

Menu's change

Recipes to celebrate

Welsh cakes and rock cakes

And bread made from sea weed

Great Welsh foods and fancies

Welsh Heritage and culture

Woollen Shawls and Welsh hats

And Welsh Lamb for me please

3. Wales versus England

No mightier bash than this

From all over Wales we gather

Trains, maybe planes, but definitely automobiles

The name has changed but the place the same

Great names

Legends we call then

Gareth, Barry, JPR AWJ, Jenkins

Davies, Edwards, we have seen them all

I can't remember the names of the English players

Never mind

Holy grass

Holy ground

The smell of the field

The roar of the crowd

Land of our Fathers trouble keeping back the tears

One united voice

Though foreign oppression lies under Welsh skies

Every hill and valley are the pride of my eyes

We sing loud and never lose our pitch

Up and down off our seats

We can't sit still

Shouts and cheers

Cwm Rhondda

Bread of Heaven

We open the roof

So, God can see us play

We always win

But when we don't

It's always the referee's fault

4. Thank you Mr. Max Boyce

From valley to valley

Town to town

Guitar in one arm and a leek in the other

A patriot of valley life

Of rugby life

Of Welsh life

Entertaining songs

Rest for miners and steel workers

Welsh valley humor

Clubs full to the brim

Duw it's hard

Slow men at work

How green was my father

So much fun and entertainment

Max you've had us in tears of laughter

We sang with you

And laughed with you

You've kept us young

We are proud to be Welsh

Thank you Mr. Max Boyce

5.   CWTCH

A bruised Knee

Time for a Cwtch

Everything is going to be OK

Creating a safe place

A heartfelt hug

A peaceful hug

Cwtch up to your Mam now

Cwtch up to your Dad now

Everything is going to be OK

6.   Our Snowdonia

Our beautiful giant

Our castle in the sky

Eryri true Welsh home

The land of the eagles

A place where eagles reign

The prince of Wales

The Lord of Snowdonia

Wild Wales

Snow peaked dreams

Natures realm played out in reality

Great Ravens Ospreys and wild birds

Echo of silence

Patient and grace

Lonely mountain calls deep within

Music of the heart in our footsteps

Upward to the pass

Beauty all around

Crib Coch

God is in the rain

Giants on the mountains

Solitude is our courtship

A noteworthy relationship

Human and nature

Harmony and respect

Rhyd Ddu

Placid and giving

Snowdonia fills our heart

May we never let her down

6, Hireath

Not easy to describe

Something we feel

Longing for the heart of love that we miss

We miss our place when we journey

Longing deep longing

Dread longing need peace

An aching groan

Depth groans of ache and absence of peace

Deep breath exhales

Missing the tender warmth of comfort and past hug

Surrounding my heart is wounded

Groan of the past distills my memory further

7.   Leaving Croesyceiliog

The wind drifts over Edlogan way

The hill steep and fierce

The people wonderful and proud

Children walk to the comp

Future being rewritten in education and fun

Stop at the shops along the way

Afon Llywd tumbles proudly by

Bryn Eglwys up we go

A pint in the Cocks on a Friday night

Walking along the Highway

Friends and fun, chants of laughter

Croesy proud, we stop and Gander

Valley steep mist covered streets

Autumn days of cool nice and fresh air

Yew tree terrace our friends all meet

Fizzy pop and chips to eat

Valley accents rise with song

Christmas soon it won't be long

For a season with change

Croesyceiliog our place to be.

8. Ashley House Cwmbran and Friday Nights

Tear away kids from all over

Fireworks and bottles of cider

Running up trappas what were we thinking

To Ashley house our Friday night fun house

Bouncy castles and kissing girls

Pop music and our latest frills

Baggy jeans and fluorescent socks

Girls with big hair and lollipops

Ashley House our Friday night venture

50 pence entry what a rip off

Too much cider we don't feel to good

Music loud and too much drama

Walking home down Trapper's hill

Through Pontnewydd and hopefully home

9. Castel Y Bwlch

A pub with good fair

Ploughman's lunch and a good pint of ale

Friendly people at the top of that hill

Great views around

The valleys we see

Finish off the meal with coffee or tea

Laughing at the bar

Old friends we do see

Memories come back

Reminisce with smiles

Atmosphere is alive

The view from the balcony is beautiful

A place to go on a summer eve

Song birds and sunsets leave us dreaming

Crimson skies and long goodbye's

The evening fades away

Castel Y Bwlch our place to go

Memories make us fonder

10. Trevethin Stands

Ancient Abergavenny Hundred

Broken spirited children play on

Community First Trevethin Stands

Pontypool it's brother

Side by side they move forward

The past is the past

The future belongs to them

Rising up the best that Wales can offer

The Folly strong and Powerful

Guarding the Welsh Valley proud

The boys are playing at top pitch

Ands we all believe in Trevethin

11. Penygarn Stores

Forget those big box stores

We're going down to Penygarn stores

Walking down Channel View

Heaven cast before us

A packet of fags and a bottle of Milk

Penygarn Stores

They've got it all

12. The Breeze blows over Pontnewynydd

Fulfilled splendours

Valleys rise up

Down hills and Traffic dictate its course

Flooding past on the way to work

Working hard

Working toil

It's a valley mans hope

Hope that work will one day end

And he rests and plays with his children

Pontnewynydd blows the breeze itself

Working for now and the future

Graft is no excuse for dreams sought

Fairy tales and hopes throughout the years

Welsh toughness and plentiful grace

Canon Lan sang in the streets

Daffydd Y Garreg Wen comes home from work

Daffydd works at motor factors

Daffydd works hard

Dreaming of a day when the sun breaks from the clouds

The rain beats down

The wind never stops

Welsh hearts and sunshine never fade

On a good day our minds are like the country

On a bad day that deep black coal

The mined coal

Slag and waste

Daffydd Y Garreg Wen gets up for work

Songs and hymns in our hearts

Valleys dreams and toil

Smoke and steam still rise from the valleys side

Children with rugby balls pass to each other

Everyone is Alun Wyn Jones

Running on the Riverside

River rolling by

The breeze blows over Pontnewynydd

13. Folly

The Folly overlooks the valley

Standing guard over the hills

Driving home we see it standing tall

Standing tall in the Eastern valleys

Bastion of a time gone bye

Touching the sky

Green valley below

Patchwork fields below

Tapestry laid out

Cwmbran, Pontypool, and more

Pristine beauty that we take for granted

Birds chirp and sing but we don't here them

Sheep bleat, robins fly

We don't see our deep Welsh green

Blessed by the rain

Hugged by the wind

We just keep on driving

We see the Folly from below

We just keep on driving

It begins to call us each day

A tower of our own hope

Calling us toward the mountain

There is a trail

A trail leads to the Folly

Beauty all around us

Birds start to tweet and chirp

Livestock roams free

We forget about our jobs

Why are we working so much?

The land is so green

We remember childhood meadows

Climbing in the trees

Running in the fields

We remember summer days

Long hot summer days

No School today

Outside for hours

Sweets and pop

Running playing and being free

Soft hills mountains and sunshine

Playing at the park

Friends giggle and laugh

Slides swings and roundabouts

Staying up late

Long summer days

Playing in the grass

Tag and Hide-and-seek

To be a child again

Green fields

A love for life

The Folly brings us home

Back to ourselves

Back to the person we had forgotten

Green fields and dry summer days

Walking up the mountain

Surrounded by paradise

At the Folly

Calling us to be ourselves

We remember lost friends

We remember ourselves

14. Abersychan Home

Not far from home where the music plays

Where rugby cheers and cries on soft black soil

Capturing the love of town and valley home

Cheers and calls to pass the ball

Cloudy skies sun peaks through

Walking with our grandfathers

Strolling down Old lane

The past is here again

Old stones rocks and hills

This valley so proud in its past

Confident that a future brings new hope

Not to distance the cries shout celebration

A Try scored for some team

Applause and shouts of praise

The wind finds its way around the terraced houses

Litter blown around

Dust off curbs

Dogs bark down some lonely street

The faintest noise of children playing in a park

Streets wet from recent rain

A touch of spring in the air

The sun burns through the cloud

Warmth becomes a welcome stranger

Valley times go slow

All good and free

15. Passion for Hills

Gilwern surrounded by the goodness of Wales

Passion for hills all around

Valley responds to matters of heart

Gilwern sinks low surrounded by the mountains

The Usk bubbles by with glints of sunshine in her streams

Curving winding filling bringing life to all she touches

Brecon canal barges steady as they go

Drifting by hello to friends

Sun shines deep warmth in our eyes

A sky so blue it hurts the eyes

Summer sun beats down on the valley floor

Grass rustles in the mid day breeze

People picnic near the canal

Cheese and cumber sandwiches crisps and cold juice

Good memories so thick we have to brush them away
from our faces

Good days and long days in Gilwern town

Friendly smiles with passer byes

Seagulls in the distance

Days like this carefree

Without worry or stress

Freedom from pain in a place called Gilwern

Leaves dance in the summer breeze

The hills smile back with pleasant glory

Green peace all around us

16. Blackrock

Mountains pierce the sky

Rain falls

Rain shadows react to the darkness

Rain it falls in sweeps and sounds

Brooks break over the Welsh black rock

Saturated ground heaves it's blanket of soil against the solid Welsh hillside

Clouds flirt with the mountain sides

Hard black rock in soil so deep

Water bounces off

No where to go

The torrent continues to drench the valley

Water floods from the rock to the villages below

We complain but it shapes us too

The rain is part of us as much as we are part of the rain

God is in the rain

He sends the rain to shape us

Let it rain let it rain let God's water fill us

Mentally rinsing us

Spiritually cleansing us

We are shaped by our mountains too

No matter where we go

Like an unseen majesty they will always be part of us

Mountains matter to the Welsh

It's where our borders begin

We are the rain

We are the black rock

Hard as rock

And soft as the soil

We are insulted the water just washes off us

We are the mountain

We are the rain

17. Cariad

Love is the heart of the Welsh

Soft and hard we can be but love is our gift

Celebration and life celebrate love

Its easy to forgive

Love is the power behind forgiveness

It's easy to love

It's hard to hate

Cariad is our word

Cariad is our hope

Cariad is our joy

18. Walking through Bwlch

Walking through Bwlch such a lovely place

The Beacons our home a place to embrace

Still yonder the black mountains stand

A pint in the New Inn

Fine Ales and good times

Farmers come down from their homes on the weekend

Enjoying the best that Bwlch has to offer

Rest and fun and catching up with friends

Welsh and English spoken a welcoming sound

19. Fallen

Sometimes we stumble

Sometimes we fail

Least is the heart who can get up again

Passion for Wales will always resound

Close by the sea

Sand blows ashore from the tempest wind

Cliffs above rocky and strong

20. CYMRU AM BYTH

This great country of ours

This lush green complexed paradise

Forever we love it

We love it for pleasure and passion

Red coloured banners fly over our streets

Green lush fields

Majestic mountains make us who we are

Being Welsh is not a birthright

It is a calling

Not to be taken for granted

Meeting on match days in our pubs and clubs

We are a fraternity of all that we hope for

Wales win

Wales lose

We are proud to be Welsh

The rain falls down

The wind blows through

Cloudy skies

Or beautiful blue

We love this place so much

Rugged coastline stretches of sand

Beauty unsurpassed around every view

Castles and towers

Ruins and churches

We all run the same race and pray Wales for ever

Welsh is unique common and free

Welsh is the tide that keeps our hearts clear

Minds eye free without pain or stress

Our identity isn't in question

We are who we are with nothing to debate

Wales for ever

Cymru am Byth

21. Patchwork Quilts

Cwmdu with its lush fields

Patchwork quilts from above

Skies are dark and stars are bright

Orion in the winter sky

Like pin holds in the curtain of night

Shining brightly over Cwmdu

What a place to live

What a time to be alive

Such beauty all around us

Existence is bliss

Once you find a place like this the wind never blows so
cold again

Patch work quilts and lush fields

Can you feel the soft winter air on your face?

Life is all around us

Do we grasp it

Or do we take it for granted

Be thankful

Or curse our lives

Orion shines brightly over Cwmdu

Sleepy village full of promise

South Wales freedom

Little children being cwtched goodnight

Everybody needs a cwtch sometimes

22. Coast

Warm breeze

Tempest Sea

Drifting surf like drizzle on the shore

Irish Sea

Tempest shore

Drizzle surfs of the drifting shore

Cool breeze

Tempest hope

Drifting drizzle shores up our likes

Welsh mountains of the sea

Waves crash against our rocky coast

Breakers billow and roll in

A surging ripple bashes the rock

Sea air deep in our lungs

Healthy hopeful for the future

Bright sky

Seagulls call

Deep green sea

Tossing its energy

A gesture of time

The sea forgives

The swell of the tide covers our past

Swn-y-Mor

The sound of the tempest

Singing in the wind

Deluge of water

Waves curl and roll

Ceridigion smiles

The Sea smiles back

The thrill of the torrent

The thrill of the surf

The roaring boisterous gale

Feeding the land with moisture

Blustering peace

Could there be such a thing as blustering peace?

Savage hope

The sea smiles at Merionydd

Merionydd smiles back

Glistening beauty

Rugged Mountains

Majestic in pose

Green dark and incredible

Merionydd still wakes

Great Wales

What an incredible country we have

Glyndwr in our hearts

Each one of us royal without prejudice

This great coast

Wales identifies shape ourselves

23. Independent

Calls for independence

We are independent already

Defined by our past

Carved by our present

Separate and devolve

In dependence

With no reason why cry

Why the need to break away

We are already different

We govern our choice

Our language is blooming

Our hope is assured

Defined and controlled

We grow stronger every day

24. Skomer

Skomer adrift in the Atlantic

Our beautiful Island

Life's full of abundance

A sanctuary to so much

Native and ancient

Birdlife and sea life call this outpost home

Burial sites of the original Britons

Atlantic puffin and Skomer vole

Boats to Skomer Island

Well worth the trip

25. West

West Wales

What a beautiful Jewel

West is best and some to adore

Walking and hiking so much to do

Hill tops and valleys coastline and sky

1000 miles of sky the land becomes our playground

Deep caves to the earths core

Bright sun and dark nights live together in freedom

Blistering heat

Frigid cold

The land so great it could be made of gold

Wheat fields and country walks

26. Tregaron

Tregaron our ancient market town

Riding the river Brenig

Broad fertile countryside

Saints still walk her streets

Fertile land and hilly regions

Eisteddfod in September

Singing song and arts

West Wallian beauty

Caron male voice choir

Singing to Heaven

27. Aberath

Aberath so close the sea

Children play and sing on fresh streets of peace

Howling winds and sheltered nights

Shipping vessels seen off the shore

Seaside village in Cardigan Bay

The wind wisps around our houses

Salt and sand chap our skin

Grass dances in the wind

Happiness is our gift

We dance in the wind too

Those blue-sky days

That help us dance away

28. Riding on the Stagecoach

Do we realise how fortunate we are?

To live in this beautiful place

If we look really hard

Lets our minds settle into peace

We will see the green of our hope

Green everywhere

Our spirit is lifted

We forget about our problems

Cool Welsh nights

Long summer days

Cwmbran, Pontypool, The Garn

Up the valley

Dance away

Up the stair case of the Eastern Valleys

Varteg, Cwmavon

Little short buses bob along

Winding roads

Up hills and down hills

Ladies out shopping

Big bags and anoraks

Blue rinse and cups of tea

Leaving Cwmbran

Off to Pontypool

Bus vibrates

Stop here please driver

The bell rings

Thanks love have a good day

Traffic calming and speed bumps

Why so many speed bumps

Edlogan way

The Highway

Driving past where rechem once stood

Remembering green smoke and strange smells

Cheap travel saying hi to friends

Jump on the stage coach

Enjoy the ride

29. Promenade

In 100 different places

100 different beeches

Promenades around Wales

White and gold sand

Stall for fish and chips

Penny slots

Cold ice cream

Fairgrounds and festivals

Miriam and Jean-Francois walk hand in hand

Sea gulls in flight above

Warm sunshine

Children play with kites

Whooshing and wooing

Bright colours in the noon day sun

Miriam buys and ice cream

French crème and chocolate

Promenades where memories and made

All over Wales

The coast is alive with good times

Friends meet and greet

Walking slowly taking it in

Bobbing in the distance

Curving through the Sea

Cutting through the surf

Sails bluster in the wind

Miriam sits on a wooden bench overlooking the beach

Children play below

Frisbees and football

A deep breath

A long exhale

The Promenade bustles with people

Nobody in a rush

Welsh coast magical majestic

Walking further

Descend to the sand

Shoes and socks off

Bare feet on the soft warm sand

Stress flows away like a mountain stream

An estuary of Peace

Promenades in Wales

Our hallowed place

Sun shines bright

Golden beach delights

30. Waterfalls

From small to large

Wales has waterfalls in every place

What could make a river run so beautifully

A sudden drop

Gushing down the rugged rock

You may forget school friends

Or people that you once know

But you'd never forget a Welsh waterfall

Lasting memory abides

Rocky crags

Tumbling falls

Lush hills and mountainsides

A rainbow

A mist driven image

Promises and priceless beauty

The torrents cascade downward

Smashing the ground with a continuing shower

The shower never stops

Time erases all things

Waterfalls help you forget

31. Irish Sea Dublin here we come

Ferry from here to there

Across the sea

The bumpy sea

Big hulking ship

Stormy sea

Bouncing up and down

Swirling wind

I'd go to the bar but not sure if I want a whiskey

Dublin here we come

Eventually

We need to get off this boat

This bumpy boat

Don't think the other passengers are too happy either

Swell and spray

Let's stay inside

I'd go to the bar but don't think I could manage a
Guinness

Passengers with green faces

How long left 2 hours

This is quite the day trip

I hate when they give storms names

Imogen storm Imogen

I know girl called Imogen once

She knocked a nun down on Brown Lane driving a Robin
Reliant

Why do they give storms names?

The sun was shining in Holyhead

This feels like a Rolla coaster

I'd go to the bar but I don't think I could mange a brandy

Can you fly to Dublin?

Next time I think we'll fly

Cary's doesn't like flying

But I don't like this bloody boat

Is it usually this windy?

I regret having that Happy Meal

I don't feel very happy now

Dublin here we come

Eventually

32. Fresh Air

Fresh Air

We've got lots of it

Meadows and hillsides

Valleys and mountains

Lakes and rivers

Fresh Breeze and sunshine

Fortunate and blessed

We take it for granted

We take each other for granted

When it gone

When things change

We miss what we have now

Fresh air friends and family

The sun shines on the hillsides

The world is a better place than we think

Misty meadows

Our minds are free

Fresh air and sunshine are sometimes all we need

33. Beth am Fod yn Wahanol

Welsh

We are different

Unique is a good thing

Different land different people

The same but different

Our differences can be celebrated

Not reduced

34. Borderlands

An odd companion

A city really not a town

Close to England

But so very Welsh

Different Welsh spoken in its suburbs

Proudly Welsh

Defiantly North Wallian

Welsh Guards

Strong and united

Wrecsam or Wrexham

Wrecsam for ever

35. OWAIN

At the bottom of despair

Not even a nation

An idea to form something

To be something

Royalty without condition

Owain stands first in the line of all who consider themselves Welsh

Brave and afraid

Strong and weary

A new path

Who will remember his name?

Will generations past remember his legacy

Rebellion was not his intention

To be freely called Welsh was his only desire

To choose a path other than one chosen for him

To dictate his own future

And that others may have the same choices as he

And from his desire

A new spirit appeared

That same spirit remains in us today

Sometimes passionate

Sometimes dormant

Always there

We see the spirit of him in ourselves

If we look deep enough

We are the dragon

His struggle remains our struggle

To govern ourselves

Not from hate or might

To be free

To chose our own path

To call ourselves Welsh

Without fear of prejudice

36. Walking down

Walking down

Sometimes too quickly

Scenery so lovely

Warm valley

Steep hill down into the valley

Walking down

Good morning Mrs. Evans

Good Morning Huw

Steep valley path

Terraced homes and houses

Still smoke in the air from wood and coal

Blue skies

Deep rise

A hillside in the village on the side of a mountain

Like everywhere else in Wales

We are either walking up

Or we are walking down

We've been walking up

Up to the shops for the milk and the paper

Now we are walking down

Back home to the Tele and Snooker

Walking down back home

Pavement wobbles and tilts uneven path

The council should do something about that

Moss and weeds growing through too

Almost home

It's allotted easier walking down than up

37. Growing a nation

Wet moist moorland

Green depth of colour

Walking through hillside and woods

A primeval soup of mud and muck

Black earth soil

Beautiful grime

Lovely clay and filth

Dust clay dark Welsh soil

You could grow anything from this ground

You could even grow a nation

The roots would have to be deep

So, we would have to dig nice and deep

Once down far enough plant the nation

Make sure it has plenty of song poetry and dancing to
keep it strong

Fertilize it with good tales

From time to time place some folklore in the soil

Important that it has enough non stop rain

With a dash of occasional sunshine

The nation will grow better on a side of a mountain

Or even in a deep valley

Take care of the nation by guarding it with dragons

In order to get the best protection, the dragons should really be red

Now the nation may not grow exactly the way you may think

But the important this is that the nation does indeed grow

When the time is right the nation may flower

And every now and then will produce sweet tasting fruit

Take the seeds from the fruit and replant

Follow the steps above and repeat

Enjoy your nation

38. Chwarae Teg

Its just the way we say it

Well done fair play

How did he do

He did well, Fair play

Chwarae Teg

Fair play they did a great job

Chwarae Teg

39. Mam

A perfect name

Much more than a word

A word which means a thousand things

This word means heart

This word means Cwtch

Not mum or mom but Mam

Mam a name full of love

Mam a lifetime of memories when we were innocent

Bedtimes stories and warm past times

Calling in for tea

Mam missed so much

Kids tele she brings us our breakfast

Tucks in bed at night

Sings to us in Welsh

We cut our knee while playing Mam is there to help us

Cold days Mam keeps us warm

Hot days Mam keeps us cool

Mam encouraging and positive

Mam such a wonderful name

40. Abergavenny Book Shop

Every book dusty and fine

Generations of books

Hundreds of years

The smell of paper from times before we were born

Books piled

Books stacked

Books everywhere

Placed in sections...kind of

Books of old

Ancient books with that ancient book smell

Page turners

Curiosity adventures for 25 pence

5 books for a quid

Dusty heaven

You could get lost in here

And I think some actually have

Mrs. Evans works the till

Cash only please

None of that modern technology

Coins being counted

Books being moved

Mountains of books everywhere

Walking home with bags of books

Only spent 10 quid

What a winner

41. Ragged

Ragged valley cliff

Deep hillside

Tumbling down

Winding valley Roads

One lane highways

Curving winding dangerous to drive

Ragged valley Side

Plants and shrubs grow out of every rock

Wild grass dancing in the wind

Streams of water shelter downwards after and early
morning rain

Becoming a brook, hitting the road below

Continuing its course

Before it meets the rivers

Ragged roads

They are all over Wales

Ragged.

42. Beautiful Dark night

In mid Wales

Away from the big towns

And the endless street lights

The night becomes alive again

Like it was in the beginning without all the light pollution

Standing here in mid Wales

On a cool December night

We sit and stand

With Telescopes and binoculars

It's cold

But our skies are dark

Not many places left in the world which are so dark

The night breeze only encourages us to look up

The majesty of the heaves laid out above us

Starts and galaxies

The Milky Way dances his waltz as the night sky
entertains us with vigour

Orion sings to us and we listen

Like children listening to a lullaby

Clouds of gases and light millions of light years away

Speaking to us through the Eons directly to us here in
Wales

Venus flirts with the moon

Dancing to an age-old song

Whirling and Waltzing what a wonderful sight

The Seven Sister have made an appearance

Bunch together

Faint but beautiful

Its cold

But we love it

No clouds

No lights

Just us and the cosmos

A blanket of creation

Inviting us in to be friends

43. Myfanwy

A song for all of Wales

Stirring applauding our souls

Our hearts leap with emotional joy

Why so angry Myfanwy

With your dark and beautiful eyes

Your gentle cheeks

A song to stir a nation

Thank you for all who sing these beautiful words

Myfanwy where is the smile upon your lips

No need to blush

Where is the smile that lit my heart?

Where now are those words

That lead me to follow you

This poet golden flame of love

Beneath the mid day suns bright glow

Sings the choir ever more

And may a blushing rose of health

Dance on your cheeks for a hundred years

I forget all the words we promised

As we sing this song

Give me your hand

So, we can no longer say goodbye

So, we can no longer say goodbye

Myfanwy boed yr holl o'th fywyd

Myfanwy may your life be full and happy

44. Aberavon Beach

High tide on the beach

Aberavon beach

Overlooking Swansea Bay

Long stretch of lovely sand

Dunes nestled in the background

Beautiful lonely beach

Sitting and walking finding ourselves again

Away from the city

Taking a break from the hustle and bustle

The bristle and drain

The world has stopped even for just a moment

Waves slowly lap the shore

No storm today

Just the storm in our minds that the beach slowly heals

Drift away

Drift away from the effort and the combustion of life

The beach is simple

Not a complicated mess

Solitude, peaceful rest

Sitting on the soft sand

Pushing our feet through the sand

Sand between our toes

Looking out over the sea

The sea forgets

Gentle breeze drifts gently by

The stress oozes out of our mind

Deep breath long exhale

The sea forgets

Warm breeze lifts our spirits

We close our eyes and think of nothing

Listen to the gentle lapping of the waves on the shore

Breaking waves

Breaking down the world for us

Life becomes simpler

Love it here

Never want to leave

Laying back now

Looking up at the pristine blue sky

The challenge of life ebbs away

The sand is our bed

Relinquishing the journey of the past that got us here

Then sound of the breeze

Scattering sand grains

Scattering complexities

We renounce our crowns

We put our agenda's away

The plan has changed

We say no more rat race

Just drifting away

On Aberavon Beach

45. TWP

Some people are Twp

Not because they are twp

But because they do twp things

Some people are called twp

But they not twp as you might think

Nobody is really twp

Like I said they just to twp things

46. Nant Trecastle

A lonesome brook

Meanders through the valley

On it's way to Trecastle

Surrounded by hillside moat and glen

Green valley

Tumbling waters

Bubbling brook continues its path

Children play in the nant

Cool fresh water

Bubbles over

Slippery rocks

Mountain water

Wonderful mountain water

Good enough to drink

Skipping stones

Fishing but nothing is biting

A lonesome brook

With children as it's companion

The creek is a salvation in the summer holidays

Kids and parents all glad that the brook is here

Easy to cool of from the sun

Giggling kids

Fun and games

Water does wonderful things for the spirit

Nant Logyn keeps on tumbling

47. Mary Jones

Its an old tale

But a good one

One that we all need to here from time to time

Faith in something bigger than ourselves

A long walk in positivity

An adventure that we all need to take

Finding the undiscovered country

Finding what we have forgotten

For Mary it was a bible

For us it could be so many other things

Following in Mary's example

Where will your journey take you?

Do you know the journey you have to take?

We all need to take the first step

And find the thing we value above all

48. Boyo

Oi Boyo

Who is the Boyo?

Wenglish noun

A young man

Even a boy

A lad

A cheeky lad

The Boyo is confident

Full of cheek and sass

A lad for the ladies

Dai bach is a boyo

So is Gwyn

A fine sense of humour comes with the boyo

Full of muck and muscle

Cheeky bugger

He'll buy you a pint though

He'll tell you ALL the jokes

Especially the ones you shouldn't here

It's good to be friends with a boyo

The boyo will watch your back

Boyo's are loyal

And even though you wouldn't think so they are loyal too

They are hard working

It's better to have a boyo on your team than 10 pressed men

Boyo's are not known for their sophisticated tastes

Steak and Kidney pie and a bag of Chips and a pint of scrumpy is the best kind of cuisine for the boyo

Nor are they known for their romantic gestures

Fancy a snog love

Is as about as romantic as it's going to get

A great night out is had with the Boyo

The life of the party

2 pints of lager and a packet of crisps

The boyo is found in every town village and city across Wales

They may have different names

In South Wales it's butty

In North Wales it's La

But a boyo is a boyo

And I'd rather be friends with a boyo

Thank anyone

49. Tears

The great flood of tears that we cried

When that day came

When that day broke

The colliery spoil tip

Broke down and fell on

21st October 1966

School just started

Kids loving life

The great flood of tears that we cried

The thunder all over the valley

Children learning for their futures

116 beautiful children

The great flood of tears that we cried

50. Glamorgan Sausage

Yum I love sausage

Nothing better than a grilled meaty sausage with egg and chips

What's in this sausage

No meat

Leek and cheese

Where is the meat

Main ingredients...breadcrumbs...OK

So, where's the meat

I'll try it

But I won't like it

Caerphilly cheese leek and Dijon

Not sure they go together

So, there's no meat

OK I'll try anything once

Yum

That's a taste sensation

That's amazing

That's the future that is

I love the cheese and leek mix

Never thought I'd say anything like that

Delicious really great

And the mustard is a perfect match

Glamorgan sausage

It's a winner

Traditional Welsh food

An awesome taste

I love it

51. Bronant

Cool winters night

Snow drifts over the hillside

Over the valley and down onto the land

Cold winter night

Darkness in the distance comes closer

The sun now set some hours before

The last ebbs of dusk mildly seen in the past

Frigid wind whisks around the village

Everyone is inside

Enjoying the warm glow of fires still lit from a flame

Doors and windows shut

The light fir the windows glows

Street lights shine on as the snow passes their light

Dancing in the wind

Large flakes of snow slowly drift downwards

From time to time a puff of a gale

Pushes itself from the heavens

Tonight, the north wind blows

A wind of change

A breath of change blows the heart

Direction headed

Passing by on the mistral of snow

A blast of cold icy wind it's the village

Trees and shrubs shake

Trying to keep the wind at bay

Like an unwelcome visitor

Barging through the doorway

The snow entices the wind

The wind delivers the snow to it's resting place

Still moving the fallen snow in wisps and shudders

The night continues

The snow falls straight down now

As the wind abates and leaves the village alone

The lure of play finesse the child in us

So seldom the snow nowadays that stays in the village

A trick to delude us maybe

Morning comes

Winter land has embraced the land

Giggly children slowly wake

As the sun comes through the curtains like a god

Curtains swept apart

Winter is here with snow and fun

A child's imagination erupts all fear

To feel free again

Against a child's innocent glow

Wellies on

Warm coats and hats

Running into the snow

Diving into the sea of white

Snowballs like projectiles invade the sky

Bronant becomes alive with laughter

The sun shines warmth on our children's hearts

And we all live again

52. Trails Trails Every where Trails

Costal path

Hillside Path

Across the mountains

Up the hills

Rugged pats

Steep and meaningful

Meaningful to the mind

Good for the soul

Rocky paths

Slow Sunday walks

Meeting friends

Hello to strangers

Where the right clothing

The weather can turn

Beautiful sunshine

Freezing rain

Kagools and Anoraks

Scenic beginnings

Walking through brooks

Always getting wet

Even the sunniest days always getting wet

Brisk walks and rosy cheeks

Over mountains and into villages

Looking of the sea

Looking over the mountain

Looking over the village

Trails everywhere

53 Kings and Castles

Rugged history

Amazing history

Our castles and forts span the nation

Where we walk

We walk the land

In the footsteps of the brave

Welsh princes and kings

The ground we tread on

Our boots press into the soil

Just as there's did so long ago

Building forts for a victory of the future

Walls and strongholds to start a nation

Broken walls completed hopes

All is good in our vales and valleys

And now we look east

For a new change

To take back what was once one

Kings and Castles

Forts and stronghold

53. I would like to take a walk

Such a nice day

I want to take a walk

Maybe to the beach

Maybe to the park

The sun is shinning and it's warm

Maybe I'll go the park

Listen to the birds chirp

Walk among the trees

Find a nice path

And just walk a while

Maybe explore

Walk to a place I've never been before

I could call it an adventure

Meet new people and see new things

I wonder where the path will take me

Enjoy the sun

The whistling wind among the trees

The leaves dance in the breeze

I'm glad I took a walk

I met some new people

Met an old friend

The walk gave me perspective

I'm glad that I went for a walk

54. No Apologies for being Welsh

Nothing to be ashamed of

Not even mentioning why

What's wrong with being Welsh

Nothing

In fact, there are allot of rights

Why do we even need this conversation?

Being Welsh is a great thing

A wonderful thing for any man of woman

Something to celebrate even

No apologies for being amazing

No apologies for being blessed

Being Welsh is a great indeed

The people wonderful

The country beautiful

No shame needed

Rich history

Glories future

No apologies needed for being Welsh

55. Cheeky Flowing River

Afon Llywd

Flowing by

Down that Welsh Valley side

Around hills

Drawing from mountains

Rocks grumble as they tumble

Bouncing of the river bed

Afon Llywd the rock breaker keeps it's nickname well

Growing in might

Falling from Blaenavon into the valley below

Smashing the coals left from years of mining

Unearthing the past

Long streams form one

Energy from the river can be heard

A hissing a none stop noise throughout the villages and
towns

Passing Garn lakes and dropping its silt

Rumbling along

A clear and present flow

Rumbling through the banks

Finding its own way

The playful glistens and weeps

Rolling in depth

Still deep and proud

Then ragged in the shallows

The sounds of the shallows change

Like a young man trying to find his way

Torfaen is his name

His name is the rock breaker

A name from memory

A river that finds it's own way

Man can't control this beast

It rambles down the valley choosing it's own path and course

Forgeside beckons it's rampant flow

As it passes children skip rocks

Pebbles bounce of the water

Children love these times

The curls of the water

The sun shines on it and it winks back at the children

Cheeky river

Flirting with Cwmavon Road

Racing towards the keepers

Only id a dream

The water so pure

The grey River

Through Ebbs and flows

Flotsam and jetson wound the river

This colt has bolted from it's mountain

Now it's free to tumble

Rumble

Continue it's path

Past the rising sun

Past Twnffrwyd

Follow the river as it bends

Along the valley floor

The river is a current of energy

Energy flows through Welsh valley life

We flow with it

We are the river

Loving the journey

Down our most wonderful valley

Twists and turns

The water flows

Ripples of Thunder

As the river becomes a torrent from the rain

The rain swells the banks

Pushing the width outwards

Engulfing soil and grass

Ripping the shore away

And making everything one

Branches and sticks bob up and down

Seeing only some on the surface

Hidden dangers below

The deluge brings new life to the giant stream

Above and below

Drifting with myself to and throw

Already at Pontypool Park

History being played out as the river dances by

A rugby match in the distance

Crowds should and call

Drifting by drifting by

Cwmbran here we come

Flooding into Croesyceiliog

Shallow paths now

Moving boulders pinching pebbles

The river burbles now

A babble and a murmur

South fields next to the river

Kids from Croesy, Pontnewydd, and Llantarnam

All collect them selves near a deep part of the river

Tire Inner tubes jumping on them

Floating down the river

Until it becomes too shallow

They get out and start again

Long summer days

The thrill of the water

Now to the boating lake

Llantarnam Jewel

Of generations of children

Enjoying the walks, the lake

Paddling boats and rowing lightly

Of large parks and helicopter play frames

Afon Llwyd stirs on

With a ripple and a patter and a peep

That cheeky flowing river continues it's course

But we are home now and time for rest

As the sun starts to set on the Eastern Valleys

We remain thankful for all the good in our lives

And we remain thankful for the Afon

As it continues it's journey without us

56. Rocky sounds

Green backgrounds

Early milk rounds

Welsh resounds

Rock pools

Rock solid

Lick your wounds

Rugby puns

Proving grounds

Compounds

Confounds

57. In memory of

Lovely green park

Mid Wales perfect

Beside a stream

Which moves gently

A park bench

Wooden and strong

Carved beautifully

Stained and dark

A sign hangs from the bench

In beautiful gold lettering

In Memory Of

Glyn and Gladys

Who enjoyed this park

This place so amazing

Sitting on the bench I take it all in

A glad vista before me

Birds sing their song without worry or care

This place is very special

A safe haven

A piece of unspoilt Glamorgan

No wind right now

Just stillness

Just total peace

From here you cannot here the hum of traffic

Or the bustle of the town

Just peaceful calm

A couple walk in the distance

Hand in hand

Walking slowly

With no hurry in their walk

Maybe the couple are Glyn and Gladys

Maybe I'm on their bench

And they are waiting to sit down and remember their lives

How amazing lives can be

So much so wonderful that someone would make a bench in loving memory of them

So serene here

The evening starts to fall

Time to go

So, Glyn and Gladys can sit on their bench

Walking slowly

With no hurry in my walk

In such a wonderful place like this

I'm so thankful for my Mam and Dad

I do miss Glyn and Gladys

I hope they like the bench I made for them

58. Welcome Home

Here we come

Over the great expanse

The hopeful bridge

Leaving England

Croeso

Below the Severn

In front of us Wales

Behind us England

We can see the valleys from here

We can see heaven from here

Lush green hills

Closer and closer

The mighty Severn Bridge

Sky and water mixed together

Yet on our canvas a wonderful tapestry

Low hill and mountain

Not a cloud in the sky

Closer now

Closer to our hallowed turf

The memories come back

Of growing up in Wales

Back in the bont

Back to the old playgrounds

Back to Mam and Dad and old friends

Back to the Bont

Where we would throw stones into the river

Rhondda we are coming home

New way Cutting through the sunlight

Love again that drifting memory

Back to Mary who waits for me

Childish dreams fill our minds

Excitement of home fills our hearts

Almost there now

Bryn Glas here soon

It will be good to be home

Good bye our bridge

Thank you for helping us get home

Now before us

The Valleys

59. Friends

Better to have friends than money

Dai, Bob, Dafydd, Jenni, Lil

All my friends are awesome

All is good

Better to have friends than money

What are you friends names

Write their names on the page

Friends will be with you in old age

When the end comes and all begins to fade

Friends will be there forever

60. Brecon Jazz Festival

Fantastic times

In the heart of the beacons

Surrounded by Gods Beauty

Surrounded by his music

That's soft progressive sound

Onlookers clap

Drinking cider

Wasps try to drink it too

The days are so warm and friendly

Great mood and cheer

Cool modern sounds

And all the saints still go marching in

Mellow and sophisticated

Brecon charm never ends

Great food great places to stay

Music that creates happiness

Myself and Ian sit in the bleachers

On our second cider and it's only 3pm

A trumpet blasts heavenly music

A man speaks with an American accent

A novel sound in a Welsh Valley

Repetitive and simple

The sound lifts the onlookers

Young men

Glance at the young ladies

The young ladies smile back and giggle

Music drifts from one place to another

Streets are pedestrianized

People walk freely hugged by sounds of hope

Dedicated venues packed to the rafters

Street performers play their clarinets and trumpets

Street music

The best in my opinion

Free and fantastic

Mistakes made but that's OK

People clap well done

Throw a few coins into the guitar case

Alternative and traditional

A lone musician on a stage

Drawing all the crowds

From a place called Memphis

So far away

Brecon Jazz Festival you have our hearts

You have our memories too

Every summer we'll take the trip

To drink cider in the sun with the wasps

And listen to the songs of our lives

Being played late into the night

61. North Wales

North Wales

Rugged and free

Peaceful with purpose

Flat and gigantic

A region it's on country indeed

Breaking the sky

Drawing the depths of the earth

Water and sky become one

Hills shout out

Here we are

Mountains shout out

We are here

Welsh homelands and heartlands

Iron Forge Wales

Strong and unapologetic

The greatest legends and stores

All have their home in this place

Stories of real people who have changed the course of Wales

North Wales

Great Wales

Standing tall in the pasture of success

Still restless for change

Promising the future realm

Steep rise

Deep fall

Like waves of rock in a Welsh ocean

Scenic valleys that will take your breath away

Visually stunning

The eyes worship the land

The land full of hope for future generations

Full of reward for the past

Rain is one with the land

Pleasant spring of heavens favour

Let it rain let it rain

Let Gods water fill us

Making us distinct from the lands around

Keeping the land green

Healthy and fertile

The people wonderful

Loving and free

Strong and mighty

Smart and loyal

And though you may not think do true royalty lives here

In the hearts and the minds of the people of North Wales

Their hearts Glow with passion

Passion for being Welsh

Songs rise from the deepest valleys

Hope rises

Discouragement and fear fall to the ground

Like a great throne that we sit upon

North Wales is our comfortable chair

Our deep lakes ripple and wash

Our deep lakes fill and inspire our dreams

We live full lives in the glow of the valley

Is it too much to ask to be truly Welsh

No to be Welsh is a great blessing

A birthright more precious than gold

North Wales our wonderful home

Our dreams become our reality

North Wales

North Wales

62. Calon Lan

It is our pure heart

It was about his

What he did for us

Saved and broken the same day

Sing in the day and in the night

True Welsh song rising from the fields from the valley
from the hillside

Lifted up so we could be lifted up

Granting us permission to sing freely

The Fair heart

That beautiful Welsh heart

An honest heart

A pure heart

63. The Welsh Woman

Welsh and proud

The Welsh Lady

The Welsh Girl

The Welsh Woman

Beautiful inside out

Carrying the dreams of her children with Celtic vigor

Her eyes gleam with sunshine

Her heart full of love

Life's battles bounce off her

Though broken she raises up her head and continues
forward

Strength beyond us

The Welsh woman is an inspiration

Depth of love in her heart never fails

She fights and wins

More precious than the most expensive gold

Though we may not always admit it

Stronger than the man she loves

The children she cares for

The Welsh woman just keeps on going

Through tough and toil, she wins the day

The Welsh woman is amazing and incredible

God bless the Welsh woman

64. Tidy

That's tidy that is

A mark of respect

Even celebration

Tidy

Even more than that

She tidy she is

At the end of the sentence

Tidy

65. Wales or England we are not sure

Monmouthshire...we think

A village and ancient village

Rockfield

Or is it LLanoronwy

Now the villagers like Rockfield

But not all of them

Some of them prefer Llanoronwy

Smack dab on the Welsh English border

Originally English

Now part of Wales

Now some of the Welsh call it Rocfield

Without the K

Some say always English

However it's beginning are actually FRENCH

Normans messing things up

In the end It matters not what the village is called

Still in Wales it is

And becoming more Welsh every day

66. Tree

Fine green tree

All over us like a friend

Dancing in the wind

Wales is known for it's trees

So beautiful our woods and forests

Chosen forests

Displaying all the colour of life

Is it easy to be free like a tree

No Cares just grow

Don't let the world rush you by

Don't let the world change who you are

Only God could make a tree

Someone once said

Take your time

Relax in your stillness

No cares just grow

Branches creek celebration in the wind

Moss grows on the bark like a warm winter coat

Snuggling warmth in chilled happiness

Bwlch-Gwyn

An other fine places

Woods and forests pictured on the forest drive

Relaxing in the still Welsh air

Water drains past them

Green hills and moss

That ancient Welsh spirit

The spirit of Kings

Lives in these trees

Ancient Kings

Ancient Welsh forests

Stretching to the sky

Reaching for hope

The sun warms the forest floor

Gives life to the carpet of foliage

Wild animals run free

Looking up to the tree for shelter

As the rain begins to fall

The tree leaves catch their downward ascent

And defer their course

When the leaves are full they let go of their cargo

Droplets hit the floor

Peace rolls over the valley

Distant thunder rolls over the sky

Everything stops and rests

Nature drinks the sky

Fine green tree

All over us like a friend

No Cares just grow

67. Weatherman Walking

Thanks Derek for showing us Wales

Walking here and there

Showing us our world

New places Old places

Places we know about

Places we didn't

Lovely to see the weatherman walking

Thank you Derek for showing us Wales

68. It's OK

It's OK

To be Welsh

It's OK

To be you

It's OK to be you

69. Our Rhondda

Our Rhondda is an amazing place

The true heart of Glamorgan

Rhondda Fawr

Rhondda Fach

Built by coal

Treherbert and Treorchy wonderful and great

Their choirs sing songs and holy to this day

Porth and Penygraig standing tall for all to see

Ystrad and Pentre all is good in this place

Cymmer still fighting the darkness of the past

Where ever you go in the world

People know the Rhondda

Mining communities of the Rhondda

A lovely place

To so many the home of Wales

The home of the Welsh

70. Pontnewydd

Walking up station road

Where the old brick bridge once stood

Now a steel bridge over Cwmbran Drive

Into the village where Dad walks

Past the Indian

Past the pharmacy

Chapel street where the Methodist church has stood for hundreds of years

Pontnewydd village

A great place to grow up

A great place to be

In Richmond Road Baptist they still sing for revival

And it will come again one day

Transforming the valleys again

At Cwmbran Rugby club

The boys have won again

Singing in the lounge

Good people Great song

A late night of fun with the best kind of people

Beer flows

And a bailey for Mr Bailey

Pontnewydd my pleasant home

Here I started

Maybe III end

Fond memories and great times

Why did I ever leave

My beautiful mountain smiles over me

Like and unseen majesty it will always be part of me

My mountain

My green hope

My Mam and Dad

My sister Trace

Pontnewydd my home

71. Coming back to Croesyceiliog

Over the train bridge

Slowly walking towards school

A journey I made for years

Walking from Pontnewydd to Croesy

A daily routine

Now the journey ends and a new one begins

I'm coming back to Croesyceiliog

Let the journey begin

-------CYMRU AM BYTH-------

Printed in Great Britain
by Amazon